The Spirit of Christmas

Nancy Tillman

FEIWEL AND FRIENDS

New York

I had just nodded off,
at a quarter past four,
when the Spirit of Christmas
stepped in through my door.

With a great show of sparkles,
he decked all my halls
in tinsel and twinkles
and bright, shining balls.

I was really quite fond of
the trimmings he'd brought.
"But there's just something
missing this Christmas," I thought.

O'er the fields we go, laughing all the way

HA HA HA

"Bells!" he said. "Jingle bells!
Bells right away! Bells on
a one-horse galloping sleigh!"

It's beginning to look a lot like Christmas!

"A toy soldier band
dressed in matching red sashes!"

"Candy cane tongues
and marshmallow mustaches!"

"Everyone caroling songs of goodwill."

"So merry that even
the trees can't be still!"

I shook my head.
"You are really so kind.
But it's just not exactly
what I had in mind."

He spoke to me then
in a whisper of wings.

"There are gentle things
the season brings."

"Snow that lies silent.

As quiet as a mouse."

"And roads that all lead to your grandmother's house."

"Ten lords a-leaping as seven swans swim."

"And of course, Santa Claus,

I'm just getting to him!"

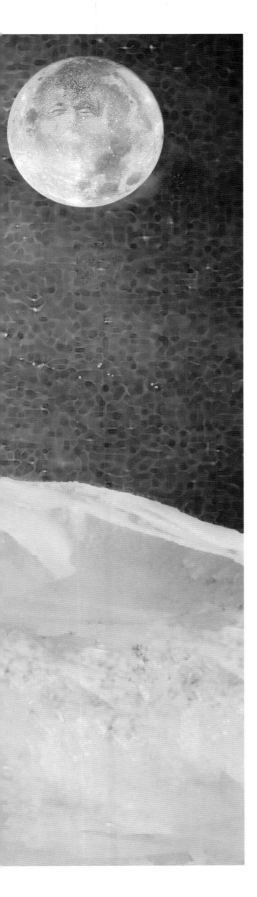

I lifted my chin
and stared up at the ceiling.
I still wasn't getting that
warm Christmas feeling.

That's when the Spirit of Christmas smiled.
"Remember, this all began with a child.
Because it took nothing but love to begin it,
it's not really Christmas if love isn't in it."

Your tree may be large as the room will allow
with a big yellow star on the uppermost bough,
but of one thing I'm certain,
I'm sure of one thing.

It is love that makes the angels sing.

And that's when I got it.
That's when I knew!
The thing that was missing
from Christmas was you!

And so then, my darling, wherever you roam,
may you always be safe…may you always come home.

For as long as the world still spins and still hums,
wherever you are, and no matter what comes,

the best part of Christmas will always be…
you beneath my Christmas tree.

For Missy, Julie, and Wes,
who danced with me around the Christmas tree.
—N.T.

A FEIWEL AND FRIENDS BOOK
An Imprint of Macmillan

Library of Congress Cataloging-in-Publication Data

Tillman, Nancy.
The spirit of Christmas / Nancy Tillman.—1st ed.
p. cm.
Summary: Despite the arrival of the Spirit of Christmas, who brings all sorts of
trimmings and reminders of seasonal joys, something is still lacking.
ISBN: 978-0-312-54965-7
[1. Stories in rhyme. 2. Christmas—Fiction. 3. Love—Fiction.] I. Title.
PZ8.3.T4545Spi 2009
[E]—dc22
2008048139

Feiwel and Friends logo designed by Filomena Tuosto
Book design by Rich Deas and Kathleen Breitenfeld
First Edition: 2009
10 9 8 7 6 5 4 3 2 1
www.feiwelandfriends.com

You are loved.